NIGHT
MONKEYS

art & words by
DANA SIMSON

A Legend Book

Andrews and McMeel
A Universal Press Syndicate Company
Kansas City

published by

Andrews and McMeel

A Universal Press Syndicate Company

Kansas City

Night Monkeys

Book Design: John Orth with Dana Simson
Typesetting Assistance: Carolyn Blakeslee and Drew Steis
The original paintings for *Night Monkeys* were rendered in highload acrylic gouache on smooth D'arches watercolor paper.

ISBN: 0-8362-1281-9

For
IMAGINATION &

D R E A M S

Special thanks to my wonderful family, the Frenchtown contingent, & "Curious George"

Night Monkeys are full
of mischief.

*Each night they leap the last
light to roll the orange sun
down the tunnel to tomorrow.*

*Kicking over pails of galaxy,
the monkeys splash out milky
puddles of distant worlds.*

They steal the planets for a game of marbles, losing Venus under a thicket of moon blossoms.

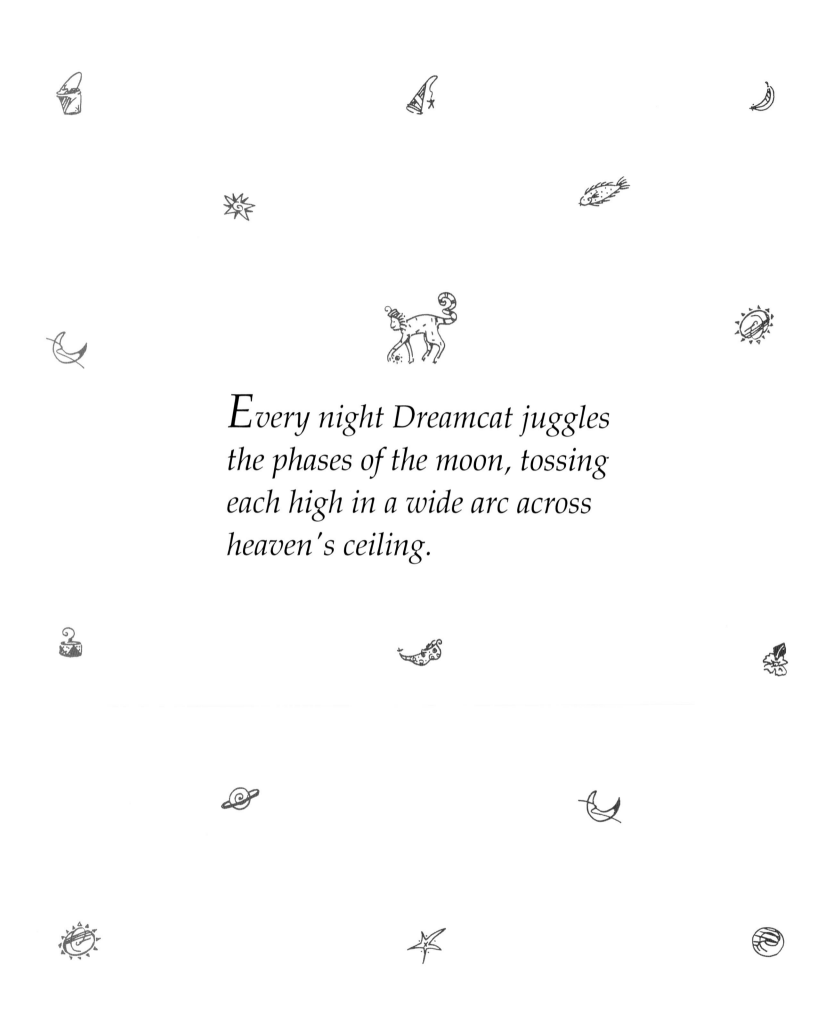

Every night Dreamcat juggles
the phases of the moon, tossing
each high in a wide arc across
heaven's ceiling.

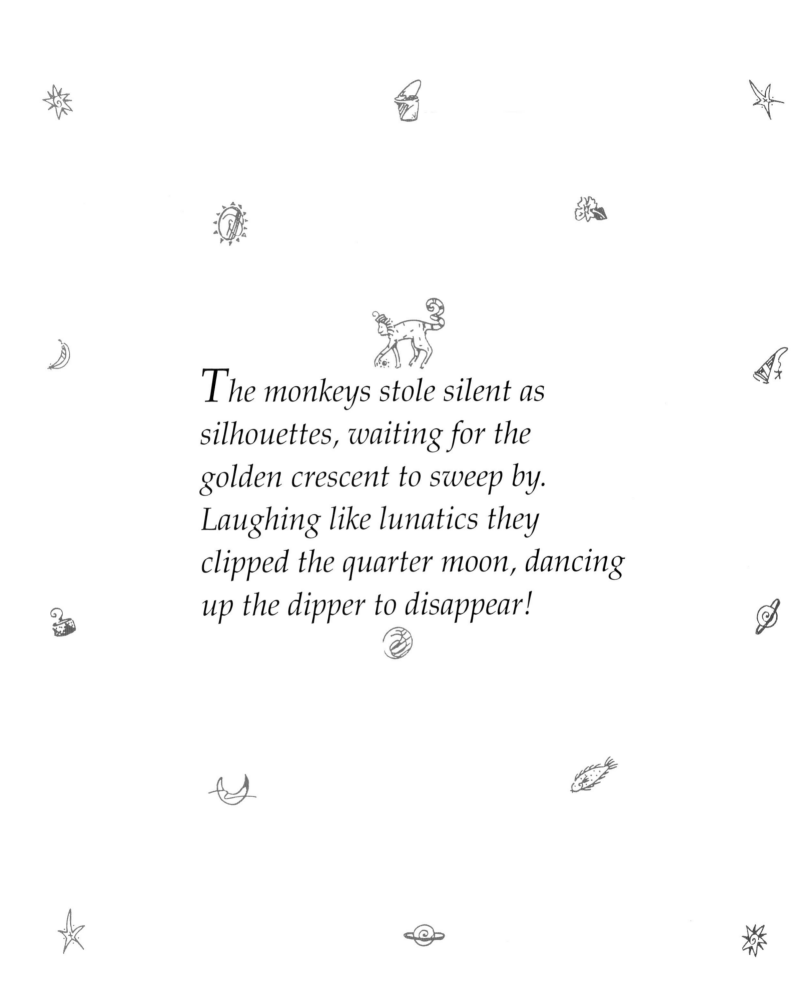

The monkeys stole silent as silhouettes, waiting for the golden crescent to sweep by. Laughing like lunatics they clipped the quarter moon, dancing up the dipper to disappear!

*D*reamcat's hand caught only
empty night. He stepped back to
let all the moons float slowly down.

In the heavens all time flows like a strong river. Nothing must get in its way and all things must be in place to receive it.

*D*reamcat caught a comet,
turning his eyes to the darkest
corners of the night where the
night monkeys slept on the
first colors of dawn.

*J*ust as the comet crested, he
blinked a bunch of bananas into
his hand, tossed them like rain
over the snoring monkeys and
bent to scoop the sliver moon
into his jacket.

*S*pinning and dropping miles to
land on all four paws, Dreamcat
rode the vapor trail home,
where the last moon was just
slipping from the sky.

The night monkeys woke later
surrounded by "banana moons."
They searched for the crescent
and were sweetly sidetracked
until they were full and forgot.

*H*e paused only to coil all
his thoughts into light and
snapped the crescent from
his hand into a beautiful
sweep across the heavens.

Dreamcat smiled and swung a
round moon over his shoulder.
It spun up like the sweetest song
casting light over each tiny world
and all creatures.